This Little Tiger book belongs to:

_____

_____

_____

for the team at
Little Tiger Press
~ L J

for Neil and Matthew
~ J P

LITTLE TIGER PRESS LTD,
an imprint of the Little Tiger Group
1 Coda Studios, 189 Munster Road, London SW6 6AW
www.littletiger.co.uk

First published in Great Britain 2001
This edition published 2014

Hide and Seek Birthday Treat

Linda Jennings   Joanne Partis

LITTLE TIGER
LONDON

Leopard wakes up with a fluttery tummy.
"It's my birthday!" he shouts with glee.
"I'm very excited, my friends are invited
to a great big party for me!"

Leopard eats breakfast, then leaves with a smile,
singing a bright birthday song.
He's going to bake a magnificent cake
for the friends he's inviting along.

Leopard goes first to his scruffy friend, Lion,
who lives in his smelly old den all alone.
There's no sound of roaring, or even of snoring.
Well Lion's not there—just a half-eaten bone!

Now Zebra lives out on the big windy plain.
Her stripes should be easy to spot.
But there on the ground, not a hoofprint is found.
Could Zebra have gone for a trot?

Surely Tiger is back in his wild woody places,
after hunting all night 'neath the moon?
But a glance in his lair shows that Tiger's not there,
even though it is now almost noon.

"Are you there, my friend Parrot?" calls Leopard.
"Don't you dare hide from me, silly bird!"
But everything's quiet where there's always a riot.
Not a squawk or a screech can be heard.

Now Peacock would be a magnificent guest,
with his many-eyed tail on display.
He's loud and he's proud—he stands out in a crowd.
But where on earth is he today?

"Is Crocodile there in the water?
He's snappy and cunning and mean.
Perhaps he is basking—I'd rather not ask him."
Even Crocodile cannot be seen!

Poor Leopard begins to feel desperate.
"Perhaps I should ask Slippery Snake?
I can't hear him hissing, don't say that he's missing.
Even he won't be sharing my cake!"

By night time it's dark in the jungle,
and Leopard pads wearily home.
It is very sad, and really too bad
he must finish his birthday alone!

But when Leopard reaches his clearing,
a very strange sight meets his eyes!
A hundred small lights burn bright in the night.
Is this Leopard's birthday surprise?

Lion, Zebra, and Tiger are waiting,
Parrot, Peacock, and Crocodile, too,
And even old Snake comes to share Leopard's cake,
and shout, "HAPPY BIRTHDAY TO YOU!"

This Walker book belongs to:

_____

_____

_____

To Alison, with love

First published 2016 by Walker Books Ltd, 87 Vauxhall Walk, London SE11 5HJ
This edition published 2017
2 4 6 8 10 9 7 5 3 1
© 2016 Petr Horáček
The right of Petr Horáček to be identified as author/illustrator of this work has been asserted
by him in accordance with the Copyright, Designs and Patents Act 1988
This book has been set in WBHoráček
Printed in Turkey by Ertem Ltd. Sti.

British Library Cataloguing in Publication Data:
a catalogue record for this book is available from the British Library
ISBN 978-1-4063-7326-4
www.walker.co.uk

WALKER BOOKS
AND SUBSIDIARIES

LONDON • BOSTON • SYDNEY • AUCKLAND

THE
GREEDY
GOAT

Petr Horáček

One Saturday morning Goat decided that she was fed up of eating herbs and grass.

She wanted to try something **new**.

First she tried the dog's food for breakfast.

It was delicious.

Especially when she washed it down
with the cat's milk.

Then Goat ate the pig's potato peelings for lunch ...

... followed by the farmer's wife's plant, topped off with one of the farmer's daughter's shoes.

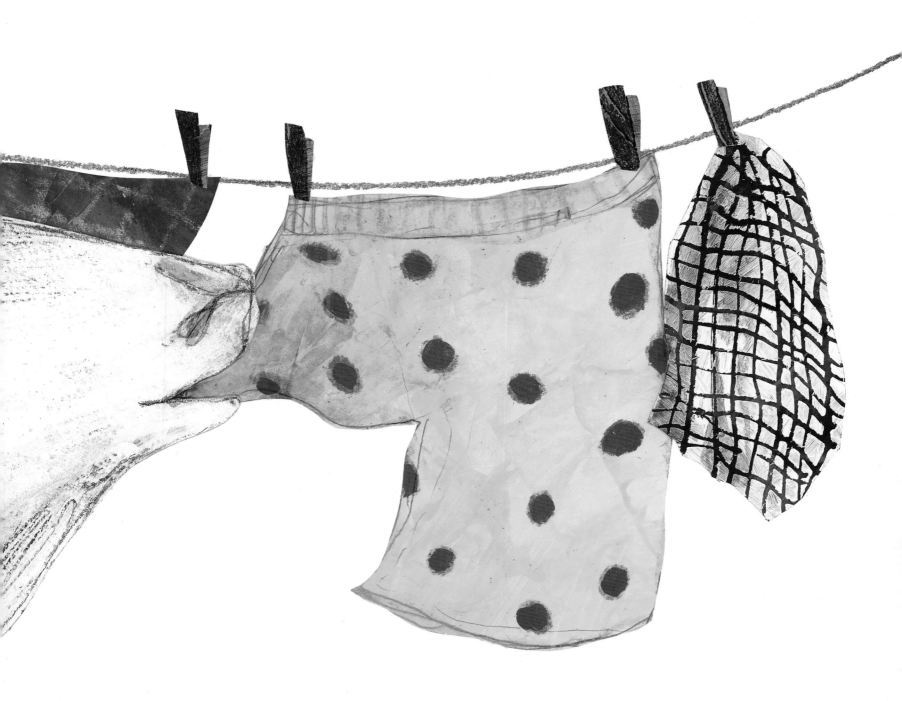

That evening she thought the farmer's pants
looked like a tasty supper.

Soon Goat didn't feel well.

She
turned
red,

blue,

yellow and green.

She went to lie down.

But her greediness
had been noticed.
"Where is my food?"
"Where is my milk?"
"Where are my potato peelings?"

"Where is my plant?"
"Where is my shoe?"
"Where are my pants?"

Everyone stopped.

"Where is GOAT?"

Goat wasn't well at all.

She was ill for the whole
of Sunday.

On **Monday** her eyes stopped rolling.

On **Tuesday** her tummy stopped rumbling.

On **Wednesday** she stopped hiccuping.

On **Thursday** she did a **huge** burp.

By **Friday** she looked almost white.

By **Saturday** the goat was herself again.

The dog got more food and the cat fresh milk. The pig had more potatoes and the farmer's wife planted a new plant.

The farmer's daughter needed new shoes and the farmer never found his pants. But at least Goat was well again.

Until she started tucking into the
farmer's wellies.

Also by Petr Horáček

978-1-4063-6601-3

978-1-4063-3776-1

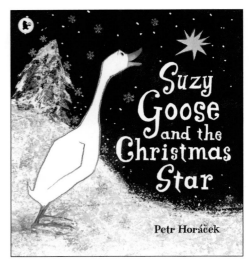

978-1-4063-2621-5

978-1-4063-0122-9

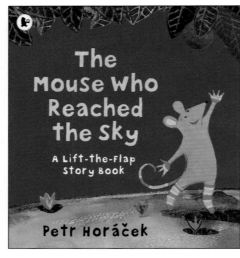

978-1-4063-6564-1

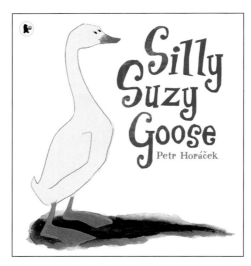

978-1-4063-0458-9

Available from all good booksellers

www.walker.co.uk